For Anna

This edition first published in the United Kingdom in 2013 by Pavilion Children's Books,
10 Southcombe Street, London, W14 0RA

Design and layout © Pavilion Children's Books 2013
Text and illustrations © Frann Preston-Gannon 2013

Associate Publisher: Ben Cameron
Designer: Claire Marshall
Commissioning Editor: Katie Deane
Production Controller: Helen Gerry

The moral rights of the author and illustrator have been asserted.

ISBN: 978-1-84365-250-2

A CIP catalogue record for this book is available from the British Library.

10 9 8 7 6 5 4 3 2 1

Reproduction by Mission, Hong Kong
Printed and bound by 1010 Printing International Ltd, China

This book can be ordered directly from the publisher online at www.anovabooks.com

PAVILION
CHILDREN'S

How to LoSe a Lemur

Frann PreSton-Gannon

Everyone knows that once a lemur takes a fancy to you there is not much that can be done about it

So when a lemur began to follow me
one bright sunny morning
in the park . . .

...I tried my hardest to ignore him.

I tried hiding up a very tall tree, but it was no good. Before long other lemurs began to appear.

So I jumped on my bike and cycled as fast as I could to try to get away.

But I wasn't fast enough.

I tried being very stern with them.
But they just smiled back at me
and wanted to play.

So I bought a ticket for
the next train leaving town.

I jumped on board
and off I went!

When that didn't work,
I jumped in a boat and
set off across the lake.

Then I took to the skies
in a hot air balloon

and floated up, UP and away.

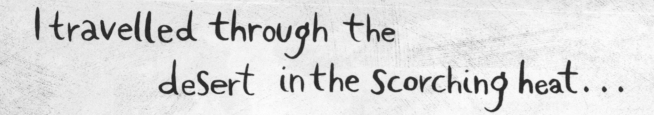

I travelled through the
desert in the scorching heat...

... But that didn't work either.

So I tried climbing the highest mountain,
through blizzardy snow and cold cold winds.

And just when I thought they had finally gone,
I realised that I had travelled very far from home
and didn't know how to get back!

I was lost and all alone.

But then, one by one, I started to see some familiar faces. They took me by the hand and we went...

back over the mountain

back through the desert

back through the skies

back across the lake

and home at last.

back on the train

And then I began to realise that maybe, just maybe, they were not so bad after all and perhaps we could be friends.

Because, as everyone knows...

... once a lemur takes a fancy to you there is not much that can be done about it.